← YOU CHOOSE →

SCOOBY-DOO!

THE GHOST OF THE BERMUDA TRIANGLE

Stone Arch Books
A Capstone Imprint

You Choose Stories: Scooby-Doo
is published by Stone Arch Books,
A Capstone Imprint
1710 Roe Crest Drive
North Mankato, Minnesota 56003
www.capstonepub.com

CAPS31132

Cataloging-in-Publication Data is available on the
Library of Congress website.
ISBN: 978-1-4342-9126-4 [Library Hardcover]
ISBN: 978-1-4342-9129-5 [Paperback]
ISBN: 978-1-4965-0105-9 [eBook]

Summary: Scooby-Doo and the Mystery Inc. gang solve
a mystery on a Bermuda Triangle cruise.

Printed in China by Nordica
0414/CA21400616
032014   008095NORDF14

What's haunting the Magical Mystery Cruise? Is it a ghost? Is the Bermuda Triangle to blame? Only **YOU** can help Scooby-Doo and the Mystery Inc. gang solve the mystery.

Follow the directions at the bottom of each page. The choices **YOU** make will change the outcome of the story. After you finish one path, go back and read the others for more Scooby-Doo adventures!

YOU CHOOSE the path to solve...

"I don't know about this, gang. Do we really want to be trapped on a boat in the Bermuda Triangle?" Shaggy moans as they walk up the gangplank.

"Reah, rit's spooky!" Scooby-Doo whimpers.

"We'll be sailing on a big cruise ship, not a boat," Velma tries to calm her friends. "And the Bermuda Triangle is just a legend."

"It's all just publicity for the cruise," Daphne assures them. "This is the Magical Mystery Cruise, after all."

"Besides, who doesn't love a free trip?" Fred reminds them. "We're lucky that the cruise line invited us because of our mystery-busting skills."

"Like, I sure hope we don't have to use them!" Shaggy worries.

Turn the page.

That night the gang goes to a costume party. The theme is Monster Mania, and everyone is dressed as a famous monster.

"Daphne, you look beautiful as the Bride of Frankenstein," Velma tells her friend. "And Fred is a great Frankenstein's monster!"

"Thanks, Velma. You sure are a great mad scientist," Daphne says. "Where are Shaggy and Scooby?"

"At the buffet table!" Fred laughs. "It's all-you-can-eat."

Shaggy and Scooby are dressed as mummies. They are wrapped entirely in bandages, except for their mouths!

"You know, pal? I'm liking this cruise now. The food is great!" Shaggy says.

"Reah! Rummy!" Scooby agrees.

"But, what's with the fake eyeballs in the Jell-O?" Shaggy wonders. Suddenly the eyes blink and move to stare straight at Shaggy. "Zoinks! They're real!"

Shaggy jumps into Scooby's arms. The two pals shiver in fear. A man stands up from behind the buffet table.

"Sorry to scare you!" he apologizes. "I'm searching for clues!"

"Like, in the fruity gelatin dessert?" Shaggy asks.

"You never know where you'll find a mystery!" the man says. He holds up a small electronic device. **BEEP!** "My ghost energy detector is on the trail!"

"R-r-rhost?" Scooby shudders.

"Eeeee!" a woman screams. It's Velma. She puts her hands over her mouth. "Oh! Did I do that out loud?" Velma looks embarrassed. "I'm such a fan of your show!"

Turn the page.

"Thanks!" the man says. He walks around the table to greet Velma. He wears a T-shirt with a *Why Files* logo on it.

"Like, who is this guy?" Shaggy asks.

"He's Max Smolder, the creator of *Why Files*!" Velma replies. "Don't you watch TV?"

"Like, only cooking shows!" Shaggy says, laughing. He goes back to the buffet table.

"Not everyone is a believer," Smolder says.

"In my experience, the truth can be really out-there," Velma says. "Are you on this cruise to investigate the Bermuda Triangle?"

"Yes! There's my crew!" Smolder points to a group of people with portable cameras. "Would you like to—"

Suddenly the lights go out! A glowing phantom appears in the middle of the room!

The ghostly shape of a man stands in the middle of the costume party guests. He is covered in dripping wet seaweed and holds a sharp trident.

"Zoinks! It's a ghost!" Shaggy gulps. "This cruise just got officially weird!"

"You passed above my watery grave!" the ghost gurgles. "Feel my revenge!"

The ghost swings the trident in circles like a crazy ninja. The party guests scream and run to avoid the weapon. Suddenly there is a stampede, and the gang is separated!

To follow Fred and Daphne, turn to page 12.
To follow Scooby and Shaggy, turn to page 14.
To follow Velma, turn to page 17.

Fred and Daphne overhear someone say there is a ghost in the cargo deck. They head down to investigate.

Standing in the very lowest level of the ship, they can feel the motion of the sea below their feet. The lights are dim and flicker off and on.

"Where's the person who reported the ghost?" Fred wonders.

"Maybe the ghost scared him away," Daphne suggests.

Suddenly they hear loud banging. It's coming from the other side of a large metal door.

"It's the ghost!" Fred gasps.

"Or maybe someone needs help," Daphne decides. She goes to the door and tries to open it. The latches don't budge. "A little help, here, Fred?"

Fred grips the metal latches and tries to turn them. He has less luck than Daphne. He steps back and shrugs.

"Heh, I guess I'm not as strong as I look," Fred says and flexes his padded Frankenstein arms.

"If brawn doesn't work, let's try brains," Daphne concludes. She reaches into her purse and pulls out a tube of lipstick.

"You look fine, Daphne," Fred says.

"It's not for me. The gloss will help loosen the locks," Daphne explains. She spreads the lip color all over the door latches. Soon the metal bolts are a lovely shade of peach.

Fred and Daphne pull the latches easily. The door swings open. They gasp!

If Fred and Daphne see a large, spooky shape, turn to page 22.
If a mysterious light glows in the doorway, turn to page 74.

"Only one thing will calm me down, Scooby," says Shaggy. "Let's go find a snack!"

Shaggy and Scooby walk into the ship's galley. It's like entering a wonderland of food. The stainless steel tables are loaded with cakes and pies, sandwiches and soups, and fresh fruits and vegetables.

"Like, we're in heaven, Scoobs!" Shaggy says, laughing. "They have everything here except Scooby Snacks."

"Rat's okay," Scooby-Doo says. He looks around at all the other tasty dishes and drools.

"Where is everybody?" Shaggy wonders. "Like, maybe the cooks are on a break."

"Rat's okay," Scooby repeats. He stares at a large stack of chocolate-covered donuts and smacks his lips.

Suddenly Scooby's nose twitches. **SNIFF!**
SNIFF! His whole body goes stiff and points like
a compass needle.

"What's up, pal?" Shaggy asks. Then his nose
twitches, too. His eyes close and his muscles go
limp.

A delicious smell wafts through the air. A
wispy stream of sweetness wraps around them.
Shaggy and Scooby lift off their feet and float in
happy bliss. **SNIFF! SNIFF!** They drift across the
galley.

The delicious scent delivers the two buddies
to a rolling table filled with desserts. Their eyes
grow as big and round as pies.

"I've never seen anything more beautiful,"
Shaggy sighs.

Suddenly something pushes Shaggy's head
into a cream pie!

Turn the page.

"Hee, hee, hee!" Scooby chuckles. He tries to look innocent.

"Mmmm! Vanilla with a hint of mint!" Shaggy says as he licks the tasty cream filling off his face. "Here, have a sample, Scoobs!"

Shaggy grabs another pie and tosses it at Scooby-Doo. **CHOMP!** Scooby catches it in his mouth and gobbles it down. Scooby throws a cupcake at Shaggy. **CHOMP!** Shaggy gulps it down.

The two pals bombard each other with every dessert they can reach. Fruit tarts fly. Sorbet soars. They throw ice cream scoops like snowballs. It's a food-for-all!

Suddenly Shaggy sees something behind Scooby that makes his eyes go wide and his mouth drop open. **PLOP!** A caramel popcorn ball lands in his mouth.

"Rwo points!" Scooby declares. Then he realizes that Shaggy is staring at something behind him. "Ruh-roh..."

If a huge shape looms behind Scooby, turn to page 18.

If a hand clamps down on Scooby, turn to page 94.

The crowd flees the threat of the ghost. People panic and run in every direction. One of those directions is smack into Velma. *THUMP!* She is knocked over, and her glasses fly off her face.

"Oh, no! I can't see anything without my glasses!" Velma moans. She gropes blindly on the floor for her eyewear.

Velma can hear the ghost ranting and the passengers screaming. She smells something stinky. *PLOP! PLOP!* Velma feels drops of goo drip on her hands. Suddenly a slimy hand grabs her arm.

"Yuck!" Velma says as she tries to pull away. "Ewww! Let go of me!"

But whatever has her won't let go. It only tightens its grip.

If Velma face drips with cold ooze, turn to page 24.
If Velma struggles against the slimy grip, turn to page 54.

Shaggy can't take his eyes off whatever is behind Scooby. "It's a monster!" he shouts. "A monster cake!" He runs toward the tower of frosting. "Like, this was for the costume party. Too bad that ghost broke up the shindig."

Suddenly the top of the cake pops open, and a sea ghost rises up from inside! The ghost drips with seaweed and ocean brine. It points a sharp trident at Shaggy and Scooby.

"Zoinks! Like, the cake is haunted! Run, Scoobs!" Shaggy yells. Their legs spin like pinwheels, but they don't go anywhere. The mess from their food fight is too slippery!

"Rit's right behind rus!" Scooby says. "Roo something!"

"I hate to do this!" Shaggy moans. He picks up a layer cake and throws it at the threatening ghost. The cake gets speared on the trident. "Aww, what a waste of a good dessert."

The ghost swings the trident, and the cake flies off the points right at Scooby-Doo. ***CHOMP!*** Scooby swallows the cake.

"Maybe it's not a waste after all!" Shaggy says, laughing.

The specter points the trident at Scooby. Shaggy knocks it aside with a giant stirring spoon.

"Nobody makes a kebab out of my pal!" Shaggy declares. He puts a metal mixing bowl on his head and grabs a pot lid for a shield. "Joust call me Sir Shaggy!"

Turn the page.

Shaggy is the picture of a brave knight in shining kitchen utensils—for about a minute. When the ghost lunges at him, the pot lid shield shakes in his hand and the mixing bowl helmet droops over his eyes. The stirring spoon sags in his grasp.

"Zoinks! So much for my career in Camelot!" Shaggy gulps.

CLANG! The ghost's trident smashes against the pot lid shield. *BANG!* Shaggy crashes up against the stainless steel wall of the galley. *CLANG!* Shaggy's armor clatters to the ground. Scooby and Shaggy hug each other.

"We're really up against the wall! This is the end, pal!" Shaggy says.

"Rou're my best friend!" Scooby whimpers.

If a small door opens behind Shaggy and Scooby, turn to page 28.

If Shaggy and Scooby try to hide in a walk-in refrigerator, turn to page 79.

"Jeepers! What's that?" Fred exclaims.

"Jeepers? Really?" Daphne puts her hands on her hips and frowns at Fred.

"Sorry. I don't have my own catch phrase," Fred grins and shrugs. "But really, what is that?"

Daphne pulls small flashlight out of her purse. The bright beam lights up a stack of cargo crates covered by a thick tarp.

"Heh, heh. Not so spooky after all," Fred says, embarrassed.

"Still, someone, or something, was banging on the door from the inside," Daphne says.

"Um, hello?" Fred shouts into the dark. "Is anybody in here?"

Fred and Daphne step cautiously into the cargo hold. The flashlight's beam does not reach very far. They stay inside its circle of light.

"Hello? Is anyone in here?" Fred repeats. The only thing he hears is the groaning of the ship's metal hull. "Well, I guess nobody's here. Let's get going."

Suddenly the door closes behind Fred and Daphne. The cargo hold goes darker than the flashlight can handle.

"Fred, please tell me that the ship shifted and made the door close," Daphne says.

"Okay. The ship shifted and—" Fred starts.

"Not what I meant!" Daphne interrupts. "We're trapped!"

If a dark shape suddenly flaps toward them, turn to page 38.

If Fred suddenly flies into the air, turn to page 91.

The cold ooze touches Velma's face. It dribbles down her cheeks like clammy drool. For a moment she thinks it's Scooby-Doo. Then someone puts her glasses on her face and she can see again! And Velma can't believe her eyes.

"Max Smolder!" Velma gasps.

"You seemed to need your glasses," Smolder says with a handsome smile.

"Thanks!" Velma says as he helps her to stand. "Um, why are you covered in goo?"

"It's ectotoplasm! The sea ghost slimed me!" Smolder replies enthusiastically. He turns to his camera crew. "Did you get that on film?"

"Sorry, boss," they shrug.

"There's no such thing as ectoplasm. It's as fake as the nineteenth-century frauds who invented it," Velma scoffs.

"Not so! There have been documented cases," Smolder disagrees.

"You mean the cases where it was proven that the ectoplasm was cheesecloth soaked in egg whites?" Velma challenges him. "Or the case where it was—"

A hideous howl is heard as the ghost rushes through the ballroom and out one of the doors.

"It's getting away!" Smolder yells. He runs after the spirit.

"Wait for me!" Velma shouts as she follows.

"I thought you didn't believe in ghosts," Smolder says.

"I said that ectoplasm is fake. I never said anything about ghosts!" Velma replies.

Turn the page.

Velma and Max Smolder chase the spooky spirit out of the ballroom and down a hallway. The lights flicker and dim as it passes. A screech rips the air.

"Wow! Light manipulation and sound generation! That's a powerful ghost!" Smolder observes, excited. He pulls a small device out of a pocket. It beeps sharply and rapidly.

"What's that?" Velma asks as she runs beside Smolder.

"It detects ghost energy!" he replies.

"Do you mean electromagnetic energy or bioelectric energy? Because there's no such thing as ghost energy," Velma states.

"You said that about ectoplasm, and yet I'm covered in it," Smolder points out.

Suddenly the specter passes through a metal door right in front of them! The device goes silent.

"No such thing, huh?" Smolder smirks.

Velma and Smolder stand in front of the large metal door. There are latches and locks on it all around the edges. Velma tries to open some of the latches but nothing budges. Smolder tries, too, and gets the same results.

"Why is this door so heavily secured?" Velma wonders.

"That's a good question for *Why Files!*" Smolder says dramatically and whistles the theme music from the show.

"Very funny," Velma says humorlessly.

"Then let's be logical. Ask yourself: Why is a ghost hiding behind a locked door?" Smolder ponders.

"If it *is* a ghost," Velma says.

"It's a ghost. I'm covered with the evidence," Smolder replies.

"I think the better question is: How do we open the door?" Velma decides.

If the ghost opens the door, turn to page **66**.
If Velma discovers the secret of the door, turn to page **69**.

Shaggy and Scooby press their backs against the wall. Suddenly a small door opens.

"Like, it's a dumbwaiter," Shaggy realizes.

"Who you calling dumb?" Scooby says.

"A dumbwaiter is like an elevator for food," Shaggy replies. "And it's our way out!"

"Geronimooooo!" Shaggy yells and jumps down the shaft.

"Scooby-Dooby-Doooooo!" Scooby says as he follows his friend.

Shaggy and Scooby tumble down the dumbwaiter shaft. They hit the sides and bounce like marbles.

The two pals come to a hard stop when they hit the top of the dumbwaiter itself. Far above them, the sea ghost screams at them from the top of the shaft. Then it starts to pull the dumbwaiter back up the shaft!

"Ruh-roh," Scooby gulps.

If they crawl out of the shaft and go through an access door, turn to page 33.

If the rope breaks and they fall to the bottom of the shaft, turn to page 67.

Daphne feels something hit her in the back. She falls to the deck and skids across the floor of the cargo hold. Daphne screams as the flashlight spins out of her grasp. Everything around her goes totally black.

"Well, now I know how Velma feels when she loses her glasses," Daphne says and tries to get her bearings in the dark.

There is a faint glow not far away. Daphne hopes it's coming from the lost flashlight. She crawls toward it on her hands and knees. The deck is filthy and greasy.

"Ewww. My party costume is ruined. And so are my nails," Daphne moans. "When this is over, I'm going to need a whole day in the ship's spa!"

Turn the page.

Daphne's hand touches something wet in the dark. It feels like a puddle of water.

"Jeepers, I hope the ship isn't leaking," Daphne worries.

Suddenly she hears the sound of something sloshing through water. She can't see it, but she can hear it coming closer and closer. Daphne's muscles freeze. Her brain can't decide if she should run or stay. Too late! Something grabs her wrist.

"Eek!" Daphne screams.

A frightening face appears out of the gloom in front of her. It looks like a human face except for the heavy eyebrows and snarling teeth. She tries to pull out of the monster's grip, but it holds on tight. She can't get away.

"I am so doomed," Daphne groans.

Turn to page 32.

"Hey, I'm just trying to help," the monster says.

Daphne blinks in surprise. She realizes that the monster is just a man. The flashlight stuffed in his shirt pocket makes his face look spooky. He lifts Daphne to her feet.

"Oh, thanks, mister," Daphne says. "Are you the person who called us down here?"

"Nope. I'm here to fix the power," the man says. "The ship has been having electrical problems ever since we sailed into the Bermuda Triangle."

Daphne's eyes adjust to the flashlight's pale glow. Now she can see that the man wears overalls and work boots.

"If you didn't call us down here, who did?" Daphne wonders.

Suddenly a terrible screeching sound hits their ears.

Turn to page 44.

"Look! There's a service door! Let's get out of here, Scoobs!" Shaggy says.

They crawl out of the dark dumbwaiter shaft and tumble into a bright room. There is a single table set with a white tablecloth, fine china, and silverware. A little old lady looks up at their sudden arrival.

"Well, it's about time you waiters got here! Where's my tea?" she demands.

"Like, sorry, ma'am," Shaggy apologizes. "We had a little detour."

"You're uniforms are . . . odd," the woman says and peers at their mummy costumes. "You must be dressed for the party upstairs."

"Yes, ma'am," Shaggy says politely. "We'll just be going back there now."

"Don't move!" the woman commands sharply.

Turn the page.

Shaggy and Scooby freeze. The woman is old and frail, but she's as scary as a skeleton! "I want my tea and dessert," she says.

Shaggy and Scooby bring plates of delicious desserts. Their mouths water at the sweet smells. Scooby's tongue reaches out for a taste. The woman whacks Scooby's nose with her napkin.

"Mind your manners!" she scolds. Scooby whimpers, but he places the plate on the table. "That's a good boy."

Suddenly a frightening figure bursts into the room. Every hair on Shaggy and Scooby stands upright. It's the ghost! They scream and hug each other. The old woman looks at the phantom and frowns.

"What are you doing here?" the woman shouts at the ghost. She smacks it with her napkin.

"Ow!" the ghost says. He pulls off his mask and rubs his head.

"You idiot! We aren't supposed to be seen together!" the old woman says. "Now these boys know who is behind the plot."

"N-no we don't! We don't know anything!" Shaggy stammers.

"My brainless accomplice was supposed to make it look like the ship was haunted and cause the cruise line to lose money," the woman confesses. "Then I would be able to buy the company at a reduced price."

"I'm sorry," the young man says and bows his head.

"You can make it up to me by getting rid of our two witnesses," the woman declares.

Turn the page.

"Throw them off the balcony and into the sea," the old lady commands. "It will be just another mysterious disappearance in the Bermuda Triangle."

"Okay," the young man says and lumbers toward Shaggy and Scooby.

"Like, this is the end, for sure!" Shaggy says. He hugs his pal.

"Rit was rice rowing rou!" Scooby whimpers.

The fake ghost grabs the pair by their mummy wrappings and shoves them toward the open balcony. The sounds of sea waves crash far below. A thick mist seeps into the room. Suddenly the fog forms a coil around Shaggy and Scooby.

"Zoinks! The mist is alive!" Shaggy shrieks.

Suddenly the lights go out! It is as if the night has come into the room. There is the sound of a struggle and then a big thud! Shaggy feels the weight of a hand on his shoulder.

"S-Scooby-Doo, is that you?" Shaggy asks.

"Rope, not me," Scooby says from the other side of the dark room.

The lights come on as mysteriously as they went off. The pals see the young man lying on the floor, unconscious. The woman is sitting, dazed, in her dining chair with a creampuff in her face.

A pale figure stands on the open balcony. He drips with seaweed and brine.

Turn to page 68.

A terrible screeching sound makes Fred and Daphne jump. Chains rattle in the dark. A large shape flaps through the air straight at them!

"Run!" Fred yells. They run, but the shape follows them.

"We need a plan!" Daphne says as she and Fred flee the flying figure.

"Split up!" Fred suggests. "It can follow only one of us at a time."

"But what if it follows *me*?" Daphne gulps.

"Don't worry, Daph. I'll make sure to get its attention," Fred assures her.

Suddenly Fred trips and falls to the deck. He slides on his stomach until he comes to a halt against one of the cargo crates.

"Um, I meant to do that," Fred mutters in a daze. "Come and get me, you murky menace."

The dark shape ignores Fred. It flaps over his head and follows Daphne. Fred tries to stand, but he is too dizzy. All he can do is watch the beam of Daphne's flashlight move rapidly away from him. Suddenly the light spins wildly and flies through the air! Fred hears Daphne scream.

"Oh, no! Daphne!" Fred moans.

To find out what happens to Daphne, turn to page **29.**
To follow Fred as he tries to help Daphne, turn to page **55.**

Velma, Shaggy, and Scooby jump up in alarm when they realize that the sea ghost is under the table with them. They accidentally knock over the buffet, and its contents go soaring into the air.

"Run!" Shaggy shouts.

The tablecloth lands on the three friends as they flee. They look like a three-headed ghost as they run blindly around the ballroom. **BONK!** They smack into a dining table. **THUD!** They stumble over a set of chairs.

"Like, who's driving?" Shaggy asks.

"Not me!" Velma replies.

"Rot re!" Scooby says. Suddenly his feet catch in the flapping tablecloth. He trips, and they all begin to fall. "Ruh-roh."

"We're doomed!" Shaggy moans. "The ghost will catch us for sure!"

Turn the page.

The friends tumble forward, tangled in the tablecloth. But instead of falling flat, they begin to roll! From the outside they look like a giant snowball. From the inside it's like being in the spin cycle of a washing machine.

"Like, I'm going to regret eating all those desserts," Shaggy moans as he turns over and over.

The sphere rumbles straight toward the sea ghost. Now it's the specter's turn to run! But there is no escape. The giant ball slams into the scary spook. The impact knocks the mask off the ghost and throws the tablecloth off of Velma's, Shaggy's, and Scooby's heads.

"Hey! I still have my glasses!" Velma says as the tablecloth lands around her. She looks at the ghost. "Hey! The ghost is a fake!"

The man in the ghost costume tries to run, but Velma grabs the trident and trips him with it. She stands over him with the tablecloth twisted around her body like a toga.

"Great Neptune!" Fred gasps as he and Daphne run into the ballroom. "Velma. you look like a sea god, er, goddess."

"You solved the mystery of the sea ghost!" Daphne exclaims.

"Not quite," Velma says. She points the trident at the man at her feet. "Explain yourself."

"I just wanted to win the costume contest," the man confesses. "I didn't mean to hurt anybody."

"He would have gotten away with it, too, if it hadn't been for Velma, Shaggy, and Scooby!" Daphne says.

"Next contest, try not to go overboard," Velma suggests.

THE END

Daphne is so startled by the sound that she jumps backward. The maintenance man's hair stands on end. He shakes in his boots. But his shaking is not from fright. Daphne sees a loose electrical wire lying in the puddle of water at the man's feet.

"Oh no! He's being electrocuted!" Daphne realizes.

"You're doomed!" a crazed voice laughs from behind Daphne.

Daphne spins around at the sound of the gloating statement. She sees a glowing figure standing on top of a stack of crates. Seaweed hangs in ragged ribbons from its rotting body. It points a trident at her.

"Prepare to meet your fate!" it cackles.

"It's the ghost!" Daphne gasps.

"H-h-help!" the maintenance man chatters through numb lips as sparks fly around his body.

Daphne turns her back on the threatening spook standing on the cargo crates. She turns her attention toward the living human being.

"I have to save him, but how?" Daphne frets. She looks at her purse.

Daphne swings the purse like an Olympic hammer-throw athlete. The handbag hits the man and knocks him out of the electrified puddle of water.

"You'll sink into the seaweed of the deepest depths!" the ghost shouts. "Sea snails will feast on your flesh! The ooze of the ages will—"

BONK! Daphne throws the maintenance man's flashlight and knocks the ghost in the noggin. His mask falls off, and he tumbles to the deck!

Turn the page.

"The sea ghost is a fake!" Daphne declares. She holds the seaweed mask in her hand.

"The sea ghost is my cousin!" the maintenance man gasps.

"It was a perfect disguise, until that meddling girl got involved," the fake ghost grumbles. "I wanted my cousin to help me steal from the cruise ship, but he refused."

"Our family has sailed these seas for generations. I won't betray their honor," the maintenance man proclaims. The two cousins argue until a misty shape covered in dripping seaweed appears between them!

"Grandpa!" the two men exclaim.

"The real ghost!" Daphne gasps. "This has to be the strangest family reunion ever!"

THE END

The device in Smolder's hands squeals like bad brakes. A black void appears in the air in front of him. Zaps of electricity flap around its edges. "Over here, Velma!"

"Jump, Max! Let's bring this kraken home," Velma says grimly as she backs toward the portal.

The monster reaches for Velma. She lets it wrap its tentacles around her. She's not afraid. She's a ghost. It can't touch her. But the kraken makes contact with the energy portal. There is a flash of lighting without thunder. There is no sound at all. The sea monster's scream is silenced.

Turn the page.

Velma and Smolder emerge from the portal and tumble across the metal deck of the cruise ship. So does the kraken! It flails its tentacles in the confined space of the cargo hold.

"Yaaa! A sea monster!" Fred yells at the sight of the beast.

"Jeepers! What's it doing in here?" Daphne shrieks.

"Daphne! Fred! Where are we?" Velma asks.

Before anyone can answer, the sea beast goes through the ship's steel hull like a phantom.

"My theory was correct!" Velma announces. "The kraken is a ghost in our dimension. It'll swim the seas as another mystery of the Bermuda Triangle."

"And I'll be there to film it!" Smolder declares.

THE END

Scooby-Doo runs and doesn't look back. He's too afraid of what he might see! In front of him is a forklift. The machine is used to move crates of cargo. The only thing important to Scooby is that it has wheels! He jumps into the vehicle and hits the gas.

"Yieeee!" Scooby yelps as the machine takes off.

The ghost leaps into a small go-cart and zooms after Scooby. Scooby zigzags all over the place. He's a terrible driver. The ghost isn't very good, either! Tires screech as both vehicles narrowly miss hitting stacks of crates and boxes. Then Scooby sees something looming ahead that makes his eyes go wide.

"Ruh-roh!" Scooby gulps.

Turn to page 51.

A huge pile of luggage blocks Scooby's escape. He shuts his eyes and crashes right through it! Suitcases go flying. The luggage pops open and clothing soars everywhere. Some of it falls down on Scooby.

"Hmm, rice routfit," Scooby says and admires the sundress and hat he now wears.

A Hawaiian shirt and a lady's skirt land on the ghost. A plastic flower lei wraps around the trident. Scooby's forklift hits a bump, and suddenly the ghost is wearing the sundress! The sun hat lands across the ghost's face.

"I can't see!" the ghost yells just before crashing the go-cart.

Turn the page.

Scooby finally finds the brakes! The forklift stops, and just in time. Fred and Daphne stand in front of the vehicle.

"What's the rush, Scoobs?" Fred asks. "Are you hot on the trail of a clue?"

"Where's Shaggy?" Daphne says. Scooby whimpers and points behind him.

"I'm over here!" Shaggy shouts. He pops up out of a big pile of clothing. "Like, look what I found!"

Shaggy holds up a ghost mask. It has a pearl necklace and a pretty silk scarf draped over it.

"Someone has some fashion sense!" Daphne declares.

Scooby-Doo digs into the mound of clothing. He comes out with the ghost!

"The ghost is a fake!" the gang says together.

"Explain yourself," Fred says sternly to the unmasked man.

"You meddling kids! My ghost disguise was supposed to scare people away from the buffet food," the man confesses.

"Why? The food's great!" Shaggy says.

"I used to be a chef with the cruise line, but I was fired unfairly. I wanted revenge," the man proclaims. "And I would have gotten away with it, too."

"Next time, just stick to a letter to the management," Shaggy says. "Come on, Scoobs. There's an all-you-can-eat buffet waiting for us!"

"Rut are re raiting for?! Scooby-Dooby-Doo!" Scooby cheers.

THE END

Velma struggles to escape the slimy hand that holds her in a death grip. Her glasses are gone, and she can't see anything! Velma is an intelligent person, but her imagination goes wild and fills with thoughts about what has a hold on her.

She is dragged through a slippery substance. Velma tries to dig in her heels to stop, but her flat shoes simply slide.

"Why didn't I choose a costume with more traction? This would not be happening," Velma laments.

"Like, you make a great mad scientist!" a familiar voice says.

Velma's glasses are placed into her palms. As soon as she puts them on, she can see Shaggy and Scooby-Doo!

Turn to page 96.

Fred scrambles to his feet. He is groggy and dizzy, but he is desperate to help Daphne. Fred stumbles across the cargo hold in the dark and keeps bumping into crates.

"Eeek!" Daphne screams. Her voice seems very far away.

"I'm coming, Daph!" Fred shouts, and trips over something in the dark. He gropes around the floor. His hands touch a shape that feels like a body. "Oh, no! Daphne!"

Fred runs his fingers along the stiff figure. Suddenly an arm falls off!

"Yikes!" Fred shrieks in alarm. "Hey, wait a minute. This isn't real. It's a statue."

Fred heaves a deep sigh of relief.

"Heh, heh. Nothing spooky about a silly old statue. In the dark. In the Bermuda Triangle," Fred tries to convince himself.

Turn the page.

Fred's eyesight slowly adjusts to the dim light in the cargo hold. He can just make out the features of the statue.

"Hey, this looks like the monster from that famous movie, *The Goblin of Green Bay*," Fred realizes. Suddenly he is more excited than frightened. "I loved that film!"

A long, low moan reminds Fred that his friend is missing. His spine goes cold. The sound seems to slither like a snake through the cargo hold. Fred drops the monster statue and runs! He can't really see where he's going. He just wants to get away from the spooky sound! But there's no escape.

"It's following me!" Fred gulps.

Fred flees blindly through the dark. **SLAM!** **SQUEECH!** He slides down the surface of a steel bulkhead like a wet noodle.

"Oooh, did anyone get the number of the truck that just hit me?" Fred moans with his face on the floor. Stars twinkle in front of his eyes. Slowly, he realizes they aren't stars. "Hey, lights . . ."

A string of low-wattage bulbs stretches along the base of the bulkhead. Fred follows the rope lights, but there is no exit.

"It's a dead end," Fred groans.

Suddenly he hears a weird sound coming from inside the bulkhead. When Fred presses his ear up against the steel wall a secret door opens. Fred falls through the opening and into a room filled with monsters!

Turn to page 84.

Lightning flashes, but there is no thunder. Velma and Smolder fall! They try to yell, but there is no sound. *THUMP!* Their feet hit the ship's deck, but it's not the cruise ship. Velma and Smolder look around in surprise and awe. Sails billow above their heads. Wooden masts creak and deck planks groan.

"We're not in Kansas anymore, Max," Velma gasps. "We're on a pirate ship!"

"Specifically, we're on the ghost's pirate ship!" Smolder declares.

The seaweed specter stands nearby, but here he is a living, flesh-and-blood man. His crewmates pay no attention to him. They all point at Velma and Max!

"Yaaar! Ghosts!" a crewman yells. "It be the Bermuda Triangle to blame!"

"Here there be monsters!" another sailor screams. He swings his sword at Velma.

The saber passes through Velma as if she
is mist. The other sailors stab at Smolder. The
blades strike air.

"We're the ghosts here!" Velma realizes.

"You're right! Listen to my ghost energy
detector!" Smolder agrees. The little device beeps
loudly.

"We stepped across a bridge in time, or
dimensions, or both!" Velma says. "That
crewman was a ghost in our world, so we're
phantoms in his!"

"I wish my camera crew was here!" Smolder
groans.

"Our ghost man brought us here, but why?"
Velma wonders.

A gigantic gurgling growl makes the pirates
fall to the deck in fear. A huge shadow crosses
over the wooden planks of the sailing ship. Velma
and Smolder look up.

"A kraken!" Velma gasps.

Turn the page.

The sinewy sea beast rises out of the water like a rearing cobra.

"T-the kraken is a m-myth!" Smolder stammers.

"Not in the Bermuda Triangle!" Velma shouts over its furious sound. "Now I know why the ghost led us here. He wants us to stop that monster!"

"How?!" Smolder squeaks.

The sea monster swipes a tentacle across the ship's deck. It goes through Velma, but it suckers onto a crewman. He is lifted into the air and then plunged into the sea.

"I have an idea!" Velma says. "Max, can your ghost detector find the energy of the doorway that brought us here?"

"Yes, but—" Smolder replies.

"Then find it and get ready to run!" Velma instructs.

Turn to page 78.

Shaggy climbs up a pile of crates like a monkey. He pauses at the top to catch his breath. That's when he realizes that Scooby isn't with him.

"Scooby-Doo, where are you?" Shaggy calls out into the vast space.

His friend doesn't answer. The cargo hold is as silent as a tomb. Then he feels a tap on his shoulder.

"Scoobs!" Shaggy says and turns. It's the sea ghost! "Zoinks! Not Scoobs!"

Shaggy jumps off the top of the crates and grabs a thick rope hanging from the ceiling. He swings away from the angry ghost.

"YaaAAAaaa!" Shaggy warbles in a bad imitation of Tarzan.

Shaggy lands in a tarp covering a pile of cargo nearby. Suddenly the heavy fabric rises up and spreads two flapping arms.

"Zoinks! Another ghost!" Shaggy shrieks. His hair stands on end!

"Scooby-Dooby-Doo!" Scooby says as he throws off the tarp.

"Pal, am I glad to see you!" Shaggy declares. Then he looks down at what Scooby is standing on. "But what is that?"

The friends stare at a big, black, shiny box. It's the size of a human corpse.

"It's a coffin!" Shaggy shouts.

The friends try to run in reverse as fast as they can. The top of the coffin is polished as smooth as glass, and their legs just spin in place.

"There's no escape, Scoobs!" Shaggy groans.

Turn the page.

Scooby-Doo accidentally trips over his own paws and falls on top of the coffin! All four of his limbs stiffen and stick out like planks. Shaggy stumbles over his friend. **SPLAT!** Shaggy and Scooby land face-first on the casket.

"Like, this is not how I want to face my final rest," Shaggy says.

Suddenly the coffin starts to shake violently. It rises into the air as if lifted by an invisible hand.

"Rit's the rhost!" Scooby yells.

The friends slide off the coffin. It crashes to the deck and breaks open. Shaggy and Scooby are amazed by what falls out!

"Rit's . . . rit's . . ." Scooby stammers.

"It's treasure!" Shaggy gasps. He gazes at the gems and jewelry spread all around his feet. "But what's it doing in this coffin?"

The only answer Shaggy gets is a terrible screeching sound. It's the sea ghost! The phantom races toward the pals with the deadly trident pointed right at them. The gleaming tips swish past Shaggy's nose. **THUNK!** The weapon gets stuck in the open coffin lid.

"Like, let's make like a dozen eggs and beat it!" Shaggy shouts.

The friends try to make tracks but their feet slip on the loose gemstones. Diamonds and rubies and emeralds go flying through the air.

Turn to page 72.

Velma and Smolder stand in front of the locked metal door. They stare at it, trying to think of a way to open it.

"It's too bad I'm not a ghost. I'd be able to pass right through it," Velma jokes.

Suddenly a pair of pale hands pokes out of the door. They are covered in dripping seaweed. Smolder's ghost detector device beeps wildly! The hands turn the latches and locks and the door swings open.

"Be careful what you wish for," Velma gulps.

The other side of the doorway is as black as the deepest night. That doesn't stop Velma or Max Smolder. They step through the portal.

Turn to page 58.

Shaggy and Scooby sit on top of the dumbwaiter as the sea ghost pulls them up the shaft.

"We're doomed," Shaggy moans.

But the weight of the two pals is too much for the rope to hold. It breaks!

"Yaaaa!" they yell as they fall all the way to the bottom. They land with a crash and tumble out of the shaft. At first Shaggy and Scooby see stars, but then they see piles of crates all around them.

"Like, we're in the cargo hold," Shaggy realizes.

"Rit's spooky rin here," Scooby shivers.

SCREEEEECCH! A horrible sound makes the pals jump. The sea ghost has caught up to them! It crawls out of the dumbwaiter shaft toward Shaggy and Scooby.

"Run!" Shaggy shouts. They flee in opposite directions.

If the ghost goes after Scooby, turn to page 49.

If the ghost chases Shaggy, turn to page 62.

"I-it's a real g-ghost!" Shaggy shudders.

"Rit's arive!" Scooby howls.

Suddenly Velma bursts into the room. Max Smolder is next to her. He holds a device in his hand that beeps loudly.

"The ghost is in here!" Smolder proclaims. He and Velma stop in their tracks when they see the unmasked "ghost" on the floor.

"Just another fake," Velma says, sighing. "It's the story of my life."

"Like, there's a *real* ghost!" Shaggy insists. "He saved us from the bad guys."

Shaggy and Scooby both point toward the balcony. It's empty. There is nothing there but a little wisp of mist.

THE END

"There's got to be a way to open this door," Velma mutters. "I wish Daphne was here with her purse. She always pulls something out of the bag."

"Do you have a hairpin? We could use it to pick the locks," Smolder suggests.

"No. Sorry," Velma replies. She pulls a makeup mirror out of her pocket. "But this might shed some light on the subject."

"How is that going to—oh," Smolder stops talking as Velma uses the mirror to reflect a ray of light onto the door. The metal surface in the center wavers like water.

"It's a hologram!" Velma proclaims. "The locks around the edges are real, but the middle is an illusion."

Turn to page 71.

Before Max Smolder can say a word, Velma walks though the metal door like a ghost! She pokes her head out a moment later and grins at Smolder's astonished expression.

"What? You've never seen a disappearing act before? It's all done with mirrors!" Velma exclaims. "Come inside. You've got to see this."

Smolder steps through the door and into a room crammed with electronic equipment.

"It's a TV control room!" Smolder says.

"Yes, and the *Why Files* crew is the only TV crew on board the ship," Velma observes. She gives Smolder a suspicious look.

"Don't look at me like that! This stuff doesn't belong to my show!" Smolder protests.

Suddenly the sea ghost appears in front of Velma and Smolder and threatens them with its trident!

Turn to page 87.

The loose gems are like ball bearings under their feet. Shaggy and Scooby slip and slide! Diamonds pelt the sea ghost. *THUD! THUD! THUD!* The stones make a dull sound as they hit the ghost.

"Like, that ghost sounds solid," Shaggy realizes. "Who ever heard of a solid ghost?"

"Rat's no rhost," Scooby agrees. He spins all four feet and sends a barrage of sparkling stones at the ghost. *THUMP! THUMP! THUMP!*

"Ow! Ow! Ow!" The ghost yelps in a human voice. The faceted gems shred his costume. Bonk! A large emerald knocks off his mask!

"You're right, Scoobs! That no ghost, that's just some guy in a gruesome getup!" Shaggy says.

"I'm not just 'some guy.' I'm the world-famous jewelry thief, Mal Le Blanc!" the man announces proudly. "I was using the cruise ship to smuggle stolen gems."

Le Blanc pulls the trident from the coffin lid. "But your meddling has exposed my scheme. I can't let you live to tell the tale!"

Le Blanc rushes at them with the sharp trident. Suddenly the coffin lifts into the air and crashes in front of the jewel thief. A hideous wail echoes through the cargo hold.

"Zoinks! It's the real ghost!" Shaggy shrieks.

The thief is so frightened that he faints!

"Like, that's a twist. Usually Scoobs and I faint!" Shaggy says. "And we solved the mystery all by ourselves!"

A ghostly voice laughs.

THE END

The rim of the doorway glows with a rainbow of wavering light. The colors shimmer and sparkle.

"Ooooh, it's so pretty!" Daphne sighs.

"I'm not so sure, Daph. We are in the Bermuda Triangle, after all," Fred worries.

Daphne reaches out to touch the glimmering colors. Fred tries to grab her hand, but he's not fast enough to stop her. They hit the mysterious light together.

Instantly all the oxygen around them is sucked away. All the light disappears. Fred and Daphne think for a second that they are in outer space—without spacesuits! In the blink of an eye, it is over.

But then Fred and Daphne realize they are not on the ship!

Fred and Daphne find themselves standing in the middle of a street. The street is unlike any they have ever seen! Vehicles zoom around them, trying not to hit them. The vehicles have no wheels. They fly through the air!

"Jeepers! Where are we?" Daphne shouts in alarm.

She and Fred jump out of the path of a speeding vehicle and onto the sidewalk. But the sidewalk is unfamiliar too—it moves!

"The doorway transported us!" Fred concludes. "We're on another world!"

Fred points to the sky. Daphne looks up and sees two bright suns.

Turn to page 77.

"Ahhhh! Monsters!" someone shrieks. Fred and Daphne look around. They don't see any monsters, but they do see the alien natives of this world. A small alien points at Fred and Daphne and shrieks, "Ahhhh! Monsters!"

"It thinks we're monsters," Fred realizes.

"Jeepers, that's a switch," Daphne says.

"Don't worry, little guy . . . er, girl . . . er, whatever you are. We won't hurt you," Fred says and tries to make a friendly gesture.

The small alien screams. A larger alien smacks Fred with something that looks sort of like a purse.

"Our party costumes aren't helping." Daphne decides. "Let's get out of here!"

Turn to page 98.

Velma digs into the pockets of her "mad scientist" costume. She rummages around until she pulls out a small makeup mirror.

"Really? You're worried about your makeup now?" Smolder says.

"Watch and learn," Velma calmly replies.

Velma twists the mirror so that it catches the light of the sun. The blinding beam hits the eyes of the monster. The kraken drops its victims from its tentacles and tries to scrub the irritating light from its orbs. Then it reaches for the source.

"Now would be a good time, Max! Where's the portal?" Velma yells.

"Coming right up!" Smolder shouts. "I hope!"

Turn to page 47.

Shaggy feels something poke him in the back. It's the handle of a walk-in refrigerator. Shaggy pulls open the stainless steel door.

"In here, Scoobs!" Shaggy shouts to his pal.

The friends run into the giant refrigerator.

"Like, this fridge is bigger than my bedroom," says Shaggy. "And there's enough food for the whole cruise ship."

Shaggy and Scooby are so dazzled by the sight that they almost forget the danger behind them.

"Shut the door, Scoobs!" Shaggy shouts. They close the giant door just in time. The angry ghost bangs against the outside. Shaggy and Scooby pile crates of vegetables and fruit against the steel door to form a barricade.

"Rat rought to rop him!" Scooby says confidently.

Suddenly the door flies open!

"Ruh-roh!" Scooby gulps.

Turn to page 81.

"Like, we forgot that the refrigerator door opens outward," Shaggy realizes. "We're doomed!"

Scooby grabs a paw full of tomatoes from one of the vegetable crates. He throws them at the sea ghost. Shaggy tosses some apples and oranges.

"Here, have a few fruits and veggies with your seaweed salad!" Shaggy shouts.

The vegetables pile up on the ghost's head. Soon the stack is a foot high! Now the ghost looks more like a tropical dancer than a fearsome spook. The veggies are so heavy that the phantom cannot keep its balance. It staggers to the left. It staggers to the right.

Then, its mask falls off!

Turn the page.

"Rit's a rake!" Scooby realizes.

"Like, why am I not surprised?" Shaggy sighs.

"You've discovered my secret, but you'll never live to tell about it!" the fake ghost says. He rushes at Shaggy and Scooby with the trident.

"Zoinks! He's going to make a kebab out of us!" Shaggy yelps.

"Ri know a reat recipe!" Scooby says. He pitches pineapples, pears, and plums at the sharp points of the weapon. The prongs fill with fruit, from base to tips. Scooby grins at his creation. "Rummy!"

"There are other ways to get rid of you meddlers!" the false ghost declares, throwing the useless trident to the floor.

"This is the end, for sure!" Shaggy moans as he and Scooby hug each other goodbye. They close their eyes and wait for the end.

BONK! THUD! Shaggy and Scooby yelp at the sounds. Then they realize the noises have nothing to do with them. They pry open their eyes and see . . .

"Daphne!" Shaggy gasps. She holds a heavy frying pan. The fake ghost lies at her feet.

"I've been looking for you guys," she says. "And I think I found you just in time."

"Ooohhh, you've ruined my perfect scheme," the ghost man moans. "I wanted the Magical Mystery Cruise to fail. The cruise line fired me and I wanted revenge."

"Like, you're getting jail time instead," Shaggy observes. "And I'm getting a snack!"

THE END

Fred is ready to run for his life! Then he sees that the monsters aren't moving.

"Statues!" Fred realizes. "They're like the one I found out in the cargo hold. But what are they doing in this secret room? And what's a secret room doing on the cruise ship?"

The mystery of the monsters makes Fred very curious. He inspects the room carefully.

"I recognize these creatures. They're from my favorite movies, and they were all designed by one man!" Fred says. He sees a portrait hanging on the wall. It portrays a dignified gentleman wearing a white lab coat. "Dr. Donald Von Lamkey!"

The painting seems to smile.

"Von Lamkey has been missing for years. Everyone thinks he's dead. But could this be his secret workshop?" Fred wonders excitedly.

Thunder booms inside the room! Lightning flashes. Fred jumps so high that he almost hits the ceiling.

"Leave this place or meet your doom!" a voice demands. "These sights are not for you to see!"

"It's the ghost!" Fred shrieks. His whole body shakes as the sea spirit stands before him and menaces with his pointy trident. Fred is about to run for his life when he notices something familiar about the monster. "Hey, you're the Screaming Specter of the Seven Seas! I love that movie!"

Turn the page.

Fred's fear fades. He grabs the trident from the ghost's skeletal hands and studies it.

"This is a fantastic prop! But it's not the original. That's in a movie museum. Did you make this? Can I see the design drawings?" Fred asks.

"A-are you a fan?" the ghost stammers.

"Are you Dr. Von Lamkey?" Fred gasps hopefully.

The ghost pulls the mask from his face.

"I'm his son, Brady Von Lamkey," the man says proudly.

"It's great to meet you!" Fred says and shakes hands. "But why did you scare the ship's passengers?"

"I was testing this costume for a remake movie," Brady confesses. "Say, I can hire some extras. Do you want to be in it?"

"Yes!" Fred says. "Another monster mystery solved! And I did all by myself!"

THE END

Smolder jumps away from the sharp points. Then he sees that Velma has not moved. She still stands in front of the spirit.

"Velma! No!" Smolder shouts as he watches her deliberately step toward the barbs of the trident. Velma walks through the phantom as if it is a cloud.

"It's another hologram! See?" Velma grins and swipes her arms through the ghost. She points to one of the TV monitors on the wall. "Look. You and I are on the monitor, but the 'ghost' isn't."

Smolder studies the control board for a moment and flips a switch. The specter disappears. He presses another button, and the ghost appears on the other side of the room.

"Great CGI work!" Smolder exclaims.

"Thanks!" a voice replies. "I specialize in computer-generated imagery!

Turn the page.

Suddenly a young man appears in the room with Velma and Smolder. He wears a *Why Files* t-shirt and rushes over to shake Smolder's hand.

"Where'd you come from?" Smolder asks, surprised.

"He was hiding behind a hologram, just like the door," Velma answers. "I saw him on one of the monitors."

"The ghost is an example of my CGI skills. I only wanted to impress you, Mr. Smolder. I'm such a fan!" the man says in a rush. "Can I have a job on your show?"

"So this was all just a job audition?" Velma realizes. "Haven't you ever heard of a regular résumé?"

"A program as sophisticated as *Why Files* demands the highest technical standards!" Smolder declares. "This young man has skills we can use."

"Thanks, Mr. Smolder! Um, I'm sorry about sliming you, sir," the youngster says.

"Why don't you show me your control board? I'm curious how you stabilized the 3-D holographic matrix," Smolder says as he and his new friend bond over SFX and hi-def tech.

"Geeks," Velma shakes her head and shrugs. She leaves the secret control room to find her friends. "I guess in this case CGI means Computerized Ghost Imposter."

THE END

Fred feels something grab him by the collar of his Frankenstein costume. He is dragged off his feet and carried through the air.

"Yaaa!" Fred yells. He spins around and catches a glimpse of Daphne's flashlight beam searching for him. "I'm over heeeeere!"

Fred's voice echoes off of the steel hull of the cargo hold. It sounds as if he is in five places at once. How will Daphne ever find him?

Fred squirms. He tries to get out of his suit. If he can get out of the jacket, he can get out of trouble! But whatever has him by the collar grips it like a predator's claw!

Turn the page.

Fred twists in midair. He clutches at whatever has him by the collar. His fingers feel something skeletal.

"Yaaa! It's the ghost!" Fred shouts. His hair stands on end, and his limbs stick out like twigs in a snowman. Then his whole body goes limp and becomes a dead weight.

"Uh-oh," the ghost gulps.

Fred and the sea specter drop to the deck. **CRASH!** The two lie in a heap as Daphne rushes up with her flashlight. It lights up Fred and . . . a woman!

"Jeepers! The ghost is a fake! You've solved the mystery, Fred!" Daphne says as she holds up the ghost's rubber seaweed mask.

"Explain yourself!" Daphne demands. She points the flashlight in the fake ghost's face.

"You meddling kids! You've ruined my plan," the woman grumbles. "I wanted to scare the passengers and have my revenge on the cruise line. They wouldn't hire me as a captain. They said I didn't have enough experience."

"And you would have gotten away with it, too, if your upper arm strength had been better," Fred explains. "You couldn't hold my weight."

"She'll have plenty of time to work out in the jail gym," Daphne says.

Fred pats his padded Frankenstein costume.

"Who knew that a few extra pounds would crack the case?" he laughs.

THE END

A heavy hand clamps down on Scooby's shoulder. At least, Scooby hopes it's a hand! His whole body trembles.

"R-rut ris it?" he asks Shaggy.

"It's . . . it's . . . it's," Shaggy stammers. Then he faints!

Scooby's teeth clack like a tap dancer's shoes. He gulps and slowly looks down at his shoulder. He expects to see the worst—and he does! Wet seaweed drips cold sea water over his fur. Skeleton fingers grip him like frigid spider legs. Scooby turns around to look at what's connected to these creepy things. He regrets it.

"Raaaa! Rit's the rhost!" Scooby screams. His limbs kick into survival gear. His legs spin like windmills gone wild. Scooby takes off and leaves his wits behind.

Scooby-Doo peels out like a drag racer. He zooms all around the galley and barely avoids the major cooking appliances.

Scooby spins around the rim of a giant stand mixer, swings from the hanging pot racks, and bounces off a huge mound of rising bread dough.

The ghost stands still in the middle of Scooby's riotous run and looks confused. Finally, the spook sticks out the trident and trips Scooby.

Scooby sails through the air with the grace of a bowling ball and lands in a pot of cooked spaghetti. **CLANG!** The pot bounces and spins. Noodles and tomato sauce fly! **SPLAT!** Everything lands on the sea ghost.

"Spaghetti and sushi? Rucky!" Scooby says as he looks at the mess.

Turn to page 100.

"I'm so glad to see you guys!" Velma declares. "Where are we?"

"Under the buffet table, where it's safe!" Shaggy says.

"And rummy!" Scooby says and licks his lips clean. He sits in the middle of a mound of food.

Now that Velma has her glasses, she sees that Shaggy is covered with pudding and frosting that she thought was ghost slime!

"That will teach me to draw conclusions before I see all the evidence," Velma states firmly.

"Don't feel bad. Here, have an éclair," Shaggy says and hands Velma a dainty delight.

"There's a ghost on the cruise ship! We have to investi—ooh, is that mint chocolate chip?" Velma says. "Maybe the investigation can wait for a minute."

Velma takes a bite of the puff pastry and sighs with happiness. She eats the whole thing and licks her fingers clean. Shaggy offers her another delicious dessert.

"Don't mind if I do," Velma says as she takes the sweet treat. "Here Shaggy, try a bonbon."

"Like, this is almost as good as a Scooby Snack," Shaggy says.

"I rike rese better!" Scooby proclaims with a mouthful of the confections.

The three friends happily hand each other cupcakes and candies, donuts and peach pies, sundaes and celery sticks.

"Celery sticks?" Shaggy says suddenly. He looks at the hand holding the leafy green vegetables and his eyes go as large as tortillas. The hand is dripping with rotting seaweed. "Ahhh! It's the ghost!"

Turn to page 41.

"We've got to get back to Earth! Where's that doorway?" Fred says.

"It's over there!" Daphne replies and points to a spot of sparkling air in the middle of the street.

Fred and Daphne try to run back the way they came along the moving sidewalk, but they end up running in place. An alien's pet growls at Fred and chomps down on his pant leg. Fred tries to shake off the little critter.

"Fluffy! The monster has my Fluffy!" a female alien shouts.

"This sidewalk is getting us nowhere," Daphne concludes. She grabs Fred's hand and jumps into the street!

Vehicles zoom around Fred and Daphne. Anti-collision force fields flare. Warning sirens blast.

"Talk about jumping out of the frying pan and into the fire!" Fred yelps.

"Hurry, Fred! The doorway is fading!" Daphne warns.

Fred and Daphne weave through traffic as if running an obstacle course. They jump over and slide under the flying vehicles as fast as they can.

"Kids, don't try this at home! Adults, don't do this either!" Fred warns the crowd of aliens pointing at his antics.

Fred and Daphne leap through the shimmering portal and vanish!

Turn to page 105.

The ghost rises up in the tangle of noodles. Gooey red sauce drips from head to toe. Shaggy wakes up just in time to see the shambling shape and faints again!

Scooby-Doo can't resist the temptation of so much pasta. He chomps down on the end of a spaghetti noodle and slurps!

The sea ghost spins around and around as the noodles unwind. Suddenly his mask spins right off his head. **PLOP!** The headpiece lands in the stand mixer and gets blended with the cake batter.

"Rey! Rou're a rake!" Scooby realizes.

"A rake? I'm not a garden tool!" the unmasked man says angrily. "I'm Mondo the Magnificent! The greatest magician on the Seven Seas!"

Turn to page 102.

"The Sea Ghost Trick will be my greatest illusion of all time!" Mondo proclaims. "But no one can witness the secret of how it's done. You and your meddling friend must disappear, forever!"

Mondo slices the spaghetti strands with the sharp ends of the trident. He bursts out of the cocoon and points the weapon at Scooby-Doo!

"Ruh-roh!" Scooby gulps. He tries to run, but his paws spin in circles on the slippery spaghetti noodles. The pasta piles up on the menacing magician but doesn't stop him.

"Ri'm roomed!" Scooby whimpers.

Scooby sees a stack of flat tortillas on a table and grabs them like a deck of cards. "Row about a rard trick?"

He shuffles the tortillas at Mondo as fast as he can. They smack the outlaw magician in rapid fire and force him backward. Scooby uses all four paws to fling the floury discs.

"Rour of a kind! Ri win," Scooby says.

Mondo stumbles and falls into the giant vat of cake batter. As Mondo gently churns around and around, Scooby takes a taste.

"Reeds more rugar," Scooby decides.

Turn the page.

Shaggy wakes up to discover Scooby-Doo licking his face.

"Hey, pal, it's nice to see you, too!" Shaggy laughs.

"Rit's ranilla icing! Rummy!" Scooby says.

"Congratulations on catching the culprit!" says the head of the ship's security. The rest of the gang is there, too. "You solved the mystery of the scary sea ghost."

"I did?" Shaggy gulps. "I wish I'd been there."

"Actually, Scooby-Doo is the hero of this case," Daphne says and pats Scooby on the head.

"Scoobs, you're the greatest!" Shaggy declares. "So what happened to that spooky specter?"

"He's just about to make his appearance," Velma says.

A giant cake rolls out of the oven. Mondo struggles to escape the massive sweet treat.

"Like, he's just another half-baked villain," Shaggy says.

THE END

Blackness surrounds Fred and Daphne as they travel through the space between worlds. This time they remember to hold their breath! They tumble out on the other side of the glowing doorway, and its light goes out. Fred and Daphne are left sitting in the dark.

"Uh, where are we?" Fred wonders.

"Fred, is that you?" a voice asks. It isn't Daphne.

The lights go on, and Fred and Daphne see Velma, Shaggy, and Scooby. They are in the ballroom.

"How did we get here?" Daphne asks. "We were in the cargo hold."

"We were on another world!" Fred exclaims. "At least I think we were."

"Oh, we were all right," Daphne says firmly and points at the tooth marks in his pant leg.

THE END

AUTHOR

Laurie S. Sutton has read comics since she was a kid. She grew up to become an editor for Marvel, DC Comics, Starblaze, and Tekno Comics. She has written Adam Strange for DC, Star Trek: Voyager for Marvel, plus Star Trek: Deep Space Nine and Witch Hunter for Malibu Comics. There are long boxes of comics in her closet where there should be clothing and shoes. Laurie has lived all over the world. She currently resides in Florida.

ILLUSTRATOR

Scott Neely has been a professional illustrator and designer for many years. For the last eight years, he's been an official Scooby-Doo and Cartoon Network artist, working on such licensed properties as Dexter's Laboratory, Johnny Bravo, Courage the Cowardly Dog, Powerpuff Girls, and more. He has also worked on Pokémon, Mickey Mouse Clubhouse, My Friends Tigger & Pooh, Handy Manny, Strawberry Shortcake, Bratz, and many other popular characters. He lives in a suburb of Philadelphia and has a scrappy Yorkshire Terrier, Alfie.

GLOSSARY

accomplice (uh-KOM-pliss)—someone who helps another person commit a crime

dimension (duh-MEN-shuhn)—measure of extension in one direction or in all directions

electrocuted (i-LEK-truh-kyoo-ted)—injured or killed with an electric shock

generation (jen-uh-RAY-shuhn)—the process of bringing something into being

imposter (im-POSS-tur)—someone who pretends to be something that he or she is not

innocent (IN-uh-suhnt)—not guilty

investigate (in-VESS-tuh-gate)—find out as much as possible

kraken (KRAK-ehn)—a sea monster

logical (LOJ-ik-uhl)—using careful thinking

phantom (FAN-tuhm)—a ghost

portal (PORT-uhl)—a gate or passage

publicity (puh-BLISS-uh-tee)—information given out about something to get the public's attention

trident (TRYE-dehnt)—a spear with three prongs

YOU CHOOSE JOKES!

YOU CHOOSE which punch line is funniest!

What do Scooby and Shaggy wear in the Bermuda Triangle?

a. **Bermuda shorts**

b. **Ghoul weather clothes**

c. **Boo jeans**

Why was Scooby underwater?

a. **He sank his ship and turned it into a nervous wreck.**

b. **He just graduated from lifeguard class and got his deep-loma.**

c. **He was Scooby diving.**

How did the lobster travel across the Bermuda Triangle?

a. **It took the octo-bus.**

b. **It moved from tide to tide.**

c. **It rode on a sleigh with sandy claws!**

What did Shaggy say when he swam in the ocean?

a. "Look at all my mussels!"
b. "Yuck! I think the sea weed!"
c. He didn't say anything, he just waved.

Why did Scooby and Shaggy stop playing cards on the cruise ship?

a. They heard the Bermuda Triangle was full of card sharks.
b. Scooby was tired of shuffling cards—he was "shuffle bored."
c. The captain of the ship was standing on the deck!

Why did Fred dress up as Frankenstein for the costume party?

a. He wanted Daphne to be his ghoul friend.
b. He wanted to win the best costume prize, of corpse!
c. Because Scooby's jokes put him in stitches!

LOOK FOR MORE...

← YOU CHOOSE →

SCOOBY-DOO!